Khalon was a happy boy. He loved to laugh and play. Khalon thought that everyone was his friend. He liked those people that he did not know very well or just met. All he knew was that he liked people and having fun.

Khalon was surrounded by much love because he had a big family. He had his grandmothers, his grandfathers, his aunts, his uncles, his cousins, his older sister, and his mom and dad.

A Note From the Author About This Series

This book is part of a series entitled "The Children's Challenges Series".

Each story presents a challenge that many students may experience, whether personally or through a friend. While the series of stories feature my grandchildren as the main characters, they are not biographical.

The purposes of the stories are to promote reading and to generate conversations about the challenges children face. The goal is to foster thought provoking questions through reading, listening, and discussing. The stories and questions will help children learn to analyze information and begin to apply the lessons learned to make sound decisions. The stories introduce concepts and vocabulary that may expand their knowledge and cause them to consider the application of the ideas.

Reading is the foundation of all areas of learning. In today's society it is essential that all of our students not only recall facts but also show the ability to critically analyze information they read to assist them in making sound decisions. Knowledge that can be effectively applied is a true sign of mastery.

These books may be used in the classroom or at home for independent reading. They can be read orally to a group of young students followed by guided questioning or read independently by the students followed by written responses that can be discussed orally. Teachers, parents or any coach can guide the stories.

Oral review of the questions is essential because this is where new ideas and the processing of critical thoughts may be supported and/or redirected if needed. Oral communication is critical and can be a fun learning activity. Each story presents a challenge that the student may relate to and will enjoy discussing possible solutions.

Presently, there are five books in the series:

Trying Something New

The Smallest Boy in Class

Going to the Dentist

Papa's in the Hospital

Swimming Lesson

I hope you enjoy these books as much as the kids do as they learn to deal with new issues in life and how to make sound decisions that promote healthy growth.

Dr. Virginia Davis

To order additional copies of this book, contact:
Xlibris
1-888-795-4274
www.Xlibris.com
Orders@Xlibris.com

ISBN: Softcover   978-1-7960-7937-1
        EBook   978-1-7960-7936-4

Print information available on the last page

Rev. date: 01/23/2020

Well, Khalon always knew he was the smallest person in his classroom. He thought that he was going to grow and catch up with the other kids. It was something that he thought about, but it never really bothered him.

One day while outside playing in the schoolyard, a new boy in his class started teasing him by calling him shorty, little man, baby, and squirt. Khalon never said anything back, but it did hurt his feelings.

When Khalon arrived home from school, his mom saw that he was not smiling. She immediately asked him what was wrong. Khalon said he was the smallest boy in the class and a new boy called him mean names because he was short. Khalon continued by saying that he knew he was short, but he thought he would get taller one day. Khalon told his mom the name-calling made him feel bad.

Mom knew that Khalon's feelings were hurt, so she decided to pull out some family pictures for Khalon to see. They were very special pictures of family members that Khalon knew and loved.

Mom pulled out the first picture of Cousin Hector who was over six feet tall. Mom asked Khalon if he knew that Cousin Hector was very small when he was a boy. Mom said the kids used to call him tiny. She also told Khalon that his dad was also a small boy in the first grade. Khalon's dad is five foot ten, but Khalon thought his dad was the tallest man in the world.

Before

After

Mom continued by telling Khalon she had a friend that was smaller than Khalon when she was in the first grade, and today, she is very tall. Mom said that the exciting thing about life is that it is filled with constant changes, and one of the changes is how we grow.

Khalon looked at all the pictures. He noticed the change in heights through the years as people became adults. Khalon thought that looking at the family pictures and seeing how everyone changed as they got older was fun.

Then mom introduced Khalon to a new word: *anticipation*. Anticipation means that you have something to look forward to that is going to happen. Khalon began to anticipate how much he was going to grow. Actually, as he looked at the pictures of his family, he noticed some of his favorite family members were not as tall as others.

Some of Khalon's family members were actually rather short. One of them was his favorite uncle Dennis. Uncle Dennis was a doctor and helped everyone in the family when they were sick. He was a very important person in the family. Uncle Dennis had a very pretty wife, Aunt Lucille, who was slightly taller than he was. Uncle Dennis had four children, and everyone in the family was happy when Uncle Dennis and his family came to visit.

That night, while Khalon was in bed, he began to think about all his family members and their different heights. He thought to himself that he might grow tall or he might be short. But what he decided was that whatever height he became, he sure hoped he could help people like Uncle Dennis.

When Khalon got up to go to school the next day, Mom reminded him that it was not how tall or how short he was that was the most important thing. The most important things are that you are the kind of person that wants to be helpful and that you have people who love you.

Before Khalon left for school, he asked his mom if he should say anything back to the name-caller. His mom told him that it was his decision, but it was not necessary that he responded to the name-caller. Then Khalon asked his mom what he should say if he wanted to respond to the name-caller.

While walking to school, Khalon decided that his response to the boy calling him names would be, "And I'm such a wonderful person." Khalon felt better when he left for school because he knew that he was loved by many people and that some of them were his friends at school.

Well, when Khalon got back to school, all the name-calling did not stop immediately. But Khalon ignored it because he had anticipation that, one day, he would get taller; and he also wanted to grow up and help people like Uncle Dennis. As the days went by, the name-calling happened less and less; and actually, when Khalon was called shorty, he did not even mind. It seemed that Khalon's anticipation about growing replaced any of his sad feelings about the name-calling. Khalon did not even have to give a response to the name-caller.

Activity Page

1. Name some things you know about Khalon?
2. What was it about Khalon that made the new student call him names?
3. How did Khalon feel when the new boy first called him names?
4. What does it mean to have hurt feelings?
5. Have you ever made fun of someone and hurt his or her feelings?
6. Why did you hurt their feelings?
7. How did that make you feel?
8. How do you think it made the person feel?
9. Has anyone ever made fun of you and hurt your feelings? Please share this experience.
10. Think of two good things that Khalon's mom did to make Khalon feel better.

11. What does it mean to anticipate?
12. What did Khalon anticipate?
13. Did Khalon anticipation make him feel better or worse? Why?
14. What did Kahlon decide to say to the name caller?
15. Draw a picture of your favorite short relative and be prepared to tell why you like the person so much.
16. Draw a picture of how you anticipate looking when you grow up.
17. Name some good things you anticipate happening some day.